Pleasing the Ghost

SHARON CREECH

Pleasing the Ghost

HARPER
An Imprint of HarperCollinsPublishers

Pleasing the Ghost
Text copyright © 1996 by Sharon Creech
Illustrations copyright © 1996 by Stacey Schuett

Library of Congress Cataloging-in-Publication Data
Creech, Sharon.
    Pleasing the ghost / by Sharon Creech.
        p.   cm.
    Summary: Nine-year-old Dennis, whose uncle and father died within a
year of one another, is visited by the ghost of his uncle, and together they settle
some unfinished business.
    ISBN 978-0-06-440686-4
    [1.   Ghosts—Fiction. 2.   Uncles—Fiction. 3.   Aunts—Fiction.
4. Communication—Fiction.]   I. Title.   II. Schuett, Stacey, ill.
PZ7.C8615Pl   1996   95-52280
[Fic]—dc20   CIP
                                                                                   AC

Typography by Michelle Gengaro-Kokmen
13 14 15 16 17   LP/BR   34 33 32 31 30 29 28
❖
Revised paperback edition, 2013

For the TASIS Lower School's young authors

Contents

I

WITH THE WIND

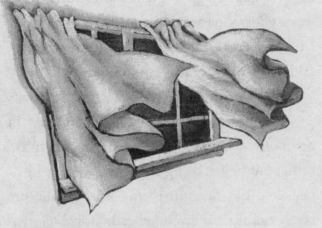

I'm Dennis, your basic, ordinary nine-year-old boy, and usually I live a basic, ordinary life. I go to school, I take care of my dog, I eat, I sleep. Sometimes, though, my life is not so ordinary. This is because of the ghosts.

Another one arrived last week. It came on the wind, like the others. It's not an ordinary wind that brings these ghosts—it's a bare whisper of wind that tickles the curtains. No one feels or hears this wind except me and my dog, Bo.

The first ghost came a month after my father died. It was my great gran, but I didn't know she was a ghost. She seemed real enough to me. When I mentioned Great Gran's visit to my mother, she said, "Dennis, Great Gran's in heaven."

"Not last night she wasn't," I said.

A month later my old cat, Choo, flew in my bedroom window. I could see him plain as anything, but he felt as light as a leaf. When I held his puckered old face up to my mother, she pressed her hand against my forehead. "Oh Dennis," she said. "Not feeling well? Choo's been dead for six months."

There have been other ghosts since Choo and Great Gran. There was an old man who used to live next door, a woman who said she had lived two hundred years ago, and a policeman. A constant parade of ghosts, but never the one I really want.

I asked the policeman ghost, "Why do ghosts visit me? Why don't they visit anyone else I know?"

"You didn't send for us? Sometimes we're sent for."

"I didn't send for you," I said. I hadn't sent for Choo or Great Gran either, though it was nice to see them. And I certainly hadn't sent for the dead old man or woman. "But if I did send for a specific ghost, would he come?"

"Hard to say," he said. "Can't always go where we aim! I was just out riding on the wind, and this is where it brought me. Thought maybe you sent for me."

Imagine! To ride on the wind and whiz into people's windows like that!

Last Friday, as I climbed into bed, I heard one of the whispering winds. When my mother came in to say good night, I asked her if a storm was coming.

"Storm? I don't think so. Look how calm it is. Not even a breeze out there."

So I knew that this was another ghost wind. Soon it would be followed by a faint whistle, and then the wind would swirl and roll and twist in through the room trailing a cloud of blue smoke. Out of that blue smoke would step a ghost. That's how it happens. It doesn't matter if the window is open or not. The wind and the ghost will come right through it.

I've tried to tell my friends and teachers about these ghosts, but they just laugh. "What an imagination!" my teachers say. One boy at school, Billy Baker, punched me in the chest. "You don't see no ghosts, you stupid liar," he said.

Billy was new at our school. My teacher sat him next to me. She whispered, "You and Billy have something in common. I know you'll be nice to him."

Nice to him! I tried, but he was the grumpiest crab I'd ever met. After he punched me for no good reason, I decided someone else could be nice to him. And as for having something in common—hah! The only things we seemed to have in common were that we were both boys and we were in the same class.

Bo whimpered in his sleep. Did he sense what was coming? The wind whistled, and the curtains curled in the air. Bo's yellow fur stood on end.

The ghosts had never hurt me, but still I was afraid. What if it was a wicked, horrible ghost? But I also wanted to know who it would be. Maybe it would be the one ghost I wanted, the one ghost I prayed for, the one ghost I'd sent for.

I had an odd, quivery feeling as that wind blew harder, reeling and rolling through the window, twisting the curtains high into the air. Bo crawled up beside me and covered his ears with his paws.

"Get ready, Bo. Here comes the ghost."

Whish! blew the wind. *Whew!* The curtains flew this way and that, knocking a book off my desk. *Whisk!* My socks lifted off the floor and danced in the air.

Bo scooted around in a circle, trying to get his

head under the covers.

Whish! Whisk! The curtains flipped into the air and sank down again, wrapping their ends around the chair. Suddenly the wind calmed. In came a quiet stream of air and a wisp of blue smoke, which swirled and floated across the room.

"Here it comes, Bo. We're about to have a visitor."

The blue smoke twisted and twirled, floating down to the floor and forming itself into a pair of green boots.

"It's here, Bo!"

The smoke formed a sturdy pair of legs in blue trousers. Next appeared a purple sweater across a big chest and arms. The smoke wiggled and wobbled and formed into a head topped by a red cowboy hat.

The ghost had arrived.

2
THE GHOST

I recognized him immediately. "Uncle Arvie! It's you, isn't it?"

"Riggle!" said the ghost, brushing himself off and rushing to hug me. His hug felt like tickling cobwebs.

It was Uncle Arvie, all right. That's just the way Uncle Arvie talks—or *used* to talk, when he was alive. Most people couldn't understand a word he said. Only his wife—Aunt Julia—and I could piece together what he was saying. But it wasn't easy.

Bo poked his nose out from under the blanket, sniffed the air, and barked. He tilted his head from side to side, staring at Uncle Arvie.

"Don't be scared, Bo. It's Uncle Arvie!"

"Yip," Bo squeaked.

"Elephant?" Uncle Arvie asked.

"No, it's my dog."

"Elephant!" Uncle Arvie insisted.

This was not going to be an easy ghost to have around.

When I was little, Uncle Arvie spoke just like everyone else, saying normal words at the normal time. But one day—when Uncle Arvie was still alive—he woke up speaking this way.

Uncle Arvie had had a stroke, and words were twisted in his brain. He knew what he *wanted* to say, but the words that came out of his mouth were not the words he chose. Sometimes they weren't even words at all—or at least not words that most people knew—like *riggle* and *fraggle*.

"You're supposed to be in heaven now," I said.

"Railroad, yin."

"Heaven—up there."

Uncle Arvie waved his arms as if he were flying. "Railroad!"

He strolled around my room, looking at things. He picked up the book that had fallen on the floor. "Pasta," he said. "Wig pasta." Next he examined the pictures on my bookshelf, picking up one of me and my mother. "Macaroni and Dinosaur!" he said.

"It's my mother and me—*Dennis*," I said.

"Macaroni and Dinosaur! Macaroni and Dinosaur!"

Uncle Arvie examined a photograph of my father and kissed the picture. "Dinosaur's pepperoni," he said. Uncle Arvie pointed toward the door. "Pepperoni?"

"My father isn't here."

"Nod pepperoni?"

"He's gone. He—"

Uncle Arvie tilted his head just like Bo, waiting for me to finish.

"He's in heaven," I said.

"Nod!" Uncle Arvie put his hands over his mouth. "Nod railroad? Nod pepperoni railroad? Nod, nod." He was very upset. My father and Uncle Arvie were brothers.

"I was hoping maybe you'd seen him there—in heaven."

"Nod, nod," Uncle Arvie cried. "Nod, nod pepperoni."

I gave him a tissue. "Last year," I said. "Right after you. He was very sick."

Uncle Arvie blew his nose.

"We miss him," I said.

Uncle Arvie held the picture to his chest.

"We miss you, too," I said.

Uncle Arvie put the picture back on the bookshelf and lifted another photograph. It was one of

Uncle Arvie and his wife, Julia.

"Oh, Heartfoot," he said. "Oh, oh, Heartfoot." He hugged the picture and kissed it.

"*She's* not in heaven," I was glad to report. "Aunt Julia's fine!"

"Oh, Heartfoot." He put the picture back and turned suddenly. "Please," he begged. "Three pleases."

"What?"

Uncle Arvie held up four fingers, looked at them, and then pushed one back down. Three fingers wiggled.

"Three what?" I asked. It looked as if Uncle Arvie wanted three things, but I had no idea what he might want. "Food?"

"Nod—"

"Money?"

"Nod, nod—"

"Clothes?"

"Nod, nod, nod—" He waggled his fingers in my face.

"Nail clippers?"

"Nod!" Uncle Arvie glanced pitifully at his fingers.

"Maybe I'll understand in the morning," I said. "You'll be here in the morning, won't you?" Some ghosts stay; some don't.

"Yin!" he said.

"Good. Then maybe we should get some sleep—"

"Stamp!" Uncle Arvie agreed. He lay down on my desk, with his long legs sticking straight out in the air over the edge, as if they were held up by something invisible. Soon he was snoring. Bo wiggled out from beneath the blanket, sniffed the air, and whimpered.

"Well, Bo, we have a new ghost! Try to be brave." I patted Bo's head until he closed his eyes.

There was no more wind. All was quiet except for the snoring of Uncle Arvie and Bo. The curtains hung straight against the window, and outside I could see the black sky and bright stars.

I found a star, and on it I wished: "Uncle Arvie is a great ghost, don't get me wrong. But still, I wish for—" I thought about what Uncle Arvie had called my father. "I wish for—for my pepperoni."

Uncle Arvie was thrashing this way and that in his sleep. He was still wearing his boots, clothes, and red hat. I was surprised that ghosts slept with their clothes on. I had thought maybe they had special white robes to sleep in.

Maybe tomorrow I could figure out what Uncle Arvie meant by "three pleases." Maybe I should tell my mother that his ghost was visiting. No. She would say that Uncle Arvie was in heaven. That there was no such thing as a ghost.

3
FIRST PLEASE

I was so scared. I was running down a railroad track, faster and faster, and there was a terrible noise behind me. I turned, expecting to see a train barreling down on me, but it wasn't a train. It was a gigantic Tyrannosaurus rex wearing a wig made of spaghetti. Someone was shouting, "Dinosaur! Dinosaur!"

I sat straight up in bed. What a nightmare. What a relief to be safe—

"Dinosaur! Dinosaur!"

Floating up near the ceiling was Uncle Arvie, calling me. Bo quivered underneath the blanket.

"Dinosaur!"

"I'm awake," I said.

"Good carpet!"

I looked down at the old, soiled carpet on my floor. It was not a good carpet at all.

Uncle Arvie stretched his arms wide and breathed deeply. "Good carpet, Dinosaur!"

"Good *morning*?" I guessed.

"Good carpet!"

Bo thumped his tail, and the blanket flopped up and down. There was a knock at my door. "Dennis? You awake?"

My heart wobbled. Would my mother be able to see Uncle Arvie? What would she say? Should I warn her?

"You're up early for a Saturday, aren't you?" she

said. Bo bounded out of the bed and leaped up against her, wagging his tail and barking. "Easy, Bo, easy," my mother said. "Looks like he's ready for a walk, Dennis. Guess you'll have to get up."

Uncle Arvie was standing behind my mother, smiling at her. "Macaroni," Uncle Arvie said. "Feather macaroni."

"Did you hear that?" I asked her.

"Hear what?"

"Do you see anything over there?"

"Sure do."

"You *do*? You actually, really and truly *do*?" I asked.

"Yes—I see books on the floor, socks in a heap. It's kind of a mess, isn't it?"

She didn't see Uncle Arvie. And yet, to me, Uncle Arvie was as clear as could be. The only difference between Uncle Arvie and my mother was that Uncle Arvie looked a little blurry around the edges.

The edges of Uncle Arvie's red cowboy hat

wobbled, as if the hat were alive. His purple sweater was slightly shimmery, almost as if it were breathing. The same was true of his trousers and boots—they shimmered at the sides, growing brighter, then dimmer.

My mother sniffed the air. "What's that smell?"

Could she *smell* the ghost?

She picked up my socks. "These should go in the wash," she said. "And there's some other smell—what is it?" She glanced around the room. "It reminds me of—of someone. I can't think who it is."

Uncle Arvie was waving his arms all around. "Pin!" Uncle Arvie said. "Pin!"

My mother dropped the socks on my bed. "Bring these down with your other dirty clothes," she said as she left.

"I don't understand it," I said to Uncle Arvie. "She can't see you or hear you, and yet I can see and hear you as clear as anything."

Uncle Arvie zoomed up to the ceiling, flipped

twice, and landed on my bed. "Three pleases? Three pleases?"

I had forgotten about that, and now that I was reminded, I was a little worried. "Let's take Bo out, and you can explain as we walk," I suggested, hurrying into my clothes.

"Pin mailer," Uncle Arvie said, flapping his arms. "Pin mailer, mailer, mailer!" He flapped his arms, lifted into the air, and sailed smoothly through the closed window.

Bo barked and jumped against the window ledge. His long tail whacked my legs. "No, Bo," I said, "you can't go through the window."

Uncle Arvie floated across the road, circled a tree, and skimmed lightly to the ground. Good thing he was wearing his green boots, because he had landed in a puddle. He stood there grinning up at us.

Bo bounded down the stairs, out the door, and stopped at the curb, wagging his tail. I led him across the street, and he leaped toward Uncle Arvie, barking and wiggling his back end. He tumbled right through Uncle Arvie and collapsed on the ground. "Yip!" he squeaked.

"One please?" Uncle Arvie said.

"I'll try," I said. "What is it?"

"Fraggle pin Heartfoot a wig pasta—"

"Wait a minute! I didn't exactly get that. Could you repeat it?"

Uncle Arvie put his hands to his eyes and formed two circles, as if he were looking through binoculars. "Fraggle pin Heartfoot—"

"Heartfoot—that's your wife, right? Aunt Julia? You want me to see her?"

"Yin!" He held his hands out, palms up, and pushed them at me.

"What? You want me to show her something?"

"Yin, yin, yin! Fraggle pin Heartfoot a wig pasta—"

For a minute there, I imagined a head covered in spaghetti, but then realized that *wig pasta* sounded familiar. Uncle Arvie had said it last night. When?

What was he looking at? "My socks?" I guessed.

"Nod, nod."

I thought again. "The book?"

"Wig pasta! Wig pasta! Yin!"

"You want me to show Aunt Julia my book?"

"Nod *Dinosaur* wig pasta. *Pin* wig pasta," Uncle Arvie said.

"You want me to show her *your* book?"

"Yin! Pin wig pasta!"

"Well, okay. Is the book at your house?"

"Yin!"

That sounded easy enough. I'd take Uncle Arvie to see Aunt Julia, and we'd find the book and show it to her. I could not imagine why this was so important to Uncle Arvie. Was there something special about the book? Would Aunt Julia be able to see her husband?

4

DEESTER IN THE WIG PASTA

On the way to Aunt Julia's, I asked Uncle Arvie why he didn't go to his house last night to see her. He spread out his arms and turned around and around and tripped and fell to the ground. "Pailandplop!"

"You couldn't steer? But how did you end up at *my* house?"

He tapped my nose with his finger. It felt as if a
fly were flapping its wings at me. "Dinosaur foodle
a doodle." Then he tapped his chest. "Pin foodle a
Dinosaur."

I couldn't make any sense out of *that*. "Will
Aunt Julia be able to see you?"

"Nod." Uncle Arvie sniffed. "Nod fraggle."

"Why not?"

"Creppit."

"Too old, huh? You think only kids can see
ghosts?"

"Yin! Foodle a doodle."

"But not *all* kids, right? Why just *some* kids?"

"Foodle a doodle—"

I still couldn't figure out what that meant, so
I said, "Couldn't *you* show her the wig pasta—the
book?"

"Nod." Uncle Arvie shook all over. "Heartfoot
twiggle a twiggle!" He trembled and looked afraid.
He opened his mouth and screamed.

Bo barked and hid behind me. "Oh, it would frighten her."

"Yin, twiggle, twiggle," Uncle Arvie agreed.

When we arrived at Aunt Julia's, Uncle Arvie leaped onto the porch. "Pin box," he said. "Pin and Heartfoot box."

"Dennis!" Aunt Julia said, opening the door. "Come on in—"

Uncle Arvie put his hands to his chest. "Oh, Heartfoot! Good carpet, Heartfoot!"

But she couldn't see him and she didn't hear him. She leaned down and kissed me and patted Bo. "I have company already," she said. "We're just having coffee."

Uncle Arvie smiled at everything he saw. He touched the walls and the furniture. He took a deep breath, as if he wanted to breathe in everything.

In the kitchen was a tall, skinny man with greasy black hair. When he smiled, I saw two silver teeth.

"Here," Aunt Julia said. "This is Colin."

"Nod!" Uncle Arvie said. "Nod a pin box! Nod beany booger—" Uncle Arvie did not like the looks of Colin. He apparently did not like another man being in his house.

"What are you looking at, Dennis? Is something wrong?" Aunt Julia said. "And what on earth is wrong with Bo?"

Bo was quivering beside me as Uncle Arvie shouted, "Nod beany booger a pin box!" I couldn't believe that Aunt Julia couldn't see or hear Uncle Arvie. He was flailing all around, shouting and waving his arms.

"Dennis? What *are* you staring at?" she repeated.

"Oh nothing—sorry," I said.

Aunt Julia sniffed the air. "What's that smell . . . ? It reminds me of . . ." She stopped and shook her head. "No, it's silly of me."

She offered me some cookies. Colin sat down and smiled his silvery smile at me and at Aunt

Julia. I didn't like the look of him either.

She brought a vase of white flowers to the table. "Look what Colin brought me. Wasn't that sweet? Don't they smell lovely?"

"Nod!" Uncle Arvie shouted. "Nod!" Uncle Arvie pushed the vase off the table. It fell with a loud crash to the floor and broke into pieces. Bo barked.

"Oh!" Aunt Julia said. "How on earth—? What happened? My goodness!"

Colin stared at the broken vase.

"Dennis, why don't you and Colin go on into the living room while I clean up this mess? I can't imagine how this happened."

In the living room, I went straight to the bookcase and looked at the titles. Which one did Uncle Arvie want me to show Aunt Julia?

Colin stood beside me. "Do you like books?" he asked.

"I guess."

"I don't, not much," Colin said. "Gives me a

headache to read a book."

"Beany," Uncle Arvie said. "Beany bud booger—"

Uncle Arvie examined the shelf. He looked and looked, at row after row of books. At last he said, "Wig pasta!" and just as he reached for a book, Colin reached up and took that same book from the shelf. "Nod!" Uncle Arvie said. "Nod pin wig pasta—"

Colin leafed through the pages. "This book would definitely give me a headache," Colin said. "The print is too small."

"Let me see it?" I said.

"Sure, just a minute. Wait, what's this?" Colin had found something in the book. It looked like a letter.

Uncle Arvie was going crazy. "Pin wig pasta a deester! Pin deester!"

Colin took the letter from the book and put it in his jacket pocket. Bo growled at Colin.

Uncle Arvie clutched his chest. "Pin deester a Heartfoot!" He pulled at Colin's jacket, trying to get the letter.

"Hey," Colin said, brushing at his jacket. "Is there something on me?"

Uncle Arvie pinched Colin's arm.

"Hey!" Colin said. "A wasp!" He took off his jacket and stomped on it.

Aunt Julia rushed in. "Why, Colin dear, whatever is the matter? A wasp? Are you okay?"

Bo dragged the jacket into the kitchen, and Uncle Arvie pinched Colin's other arm.

"Hey!" Colin wailed. "Another one?" He slapped at his arm.

"Oh goodness, goodness," Aunt Julia said.

In the kitchen Bo was scratching at Colin's jacket. "Here, I'll get it," I said. On the envelope was written, "Pin Heartfoot." I stuffed the letter into my own pocket and took Colin's jacket back to him.

Uncle Arvie must have pinched Colin again, because Colin was saying, "Hey! Hey!" Colin swung at the air and slapped at his neck. "I'm going!" he said, rushing for the door.

"Oh, goodness," Aunt Julia said.

"Aunt Julia," I said, "I was looking at one of your books and I found something. I think it's for you." I gave her the letter.

"Oh!" She kissed the envelope. "It's from Arvie!" She tore open the envelope and read the note inside. "Look," she said, "it was written the day before Arvie died." She read:

> *"Heartfoot a lalley*
> *Heartfoot a sweel*
> *Pin Heartfoot pin Heartfoot*
> *Pin Heartfoot a teel.*

"Oh, how lovely, how sweet," she said.

Uncle Arvie was staring at her.

"What does it mean?" I asked.

"Well," she said. "I'm not entirely sure. *Heartfoot*—that's me. That's what he called me after his stroke. And *pin*—that usually meant *me* or *my*. But I don't know what *lalley* or *sweel* or *teel* mean. It's still lovely, though. I'm sure it's a love poem."

Bo put his head on her foot and slobbered.

"I bet this was for my birthday," she said. "He didn't forget it after all."

She read the poem again and again. Once she looked up and sniffed the air. "That smell," she said. "Doesn't it smell like—like Arvie?"

Uncle Arvie leaned down and kissed her cheek. She couldn't see him, but she must have felt something, because she put her hand to her cheek.

"I'm feeling a little peculiar," she said. "I think I'll lie down. But thank you for finding this. I might never ever have discovered it."

I thought Uncle Arvie might stay with Julia, but he followed me and Bo out the door. He looked tired and sad.

"You miss her, don't you?" I said.

"Pin sweel Heartfoot," Uncle Arvie said.

"I didn't much like that Colin guy, did you?"

"Beany booger!"

"Exactly," I said.

We were nearly home when Uncle Arvie said, "Two please?"

I had nearly forgotten about the three pleases. I had done the first one, by finding the book with its letter and giving it to Aunt Julia. Now what would the next please be?

5

SECOND PLEASE

As we were crossing the park on our way home from Aunt Julia's house, a boy on a bike stopped us. The bike was spectacular, but the boy was not. It was Billy Baker, the one who had called me a liar when I had told him about my ghosts.

Billy Baker said, "Hey, Dennis. Is that your stinking dog?"

Bo growled a long, low, menacing growl.

"It's my dog," I said, "but he's not stinking."

"Oh yeah?" Billy said. "I bet he is."

"Beany booger?" Uncle Arvie said.

"Yes," I agreed. "A beany booger."

"What?" Billy demanded. "Who are you calling a beany booger?"

"Nobody."

"You'd better not be calling *me* that—"

Bo snapped Billy's jeans in his teeth and pulled
at them.

"Hey, get your stinking dog off me!"

"You shouldn't have called him stinking," I
said.

Bo pulled at Billy's jeans, making him lose his
balance.

"Get this dog off me!"

"Come on, Bo. Let him go."

Reluctantly, Bo let Billy loose. Billy hissed in
my ear: "You'll be sorry for this! I'll catch you
sometime when you don't have your stinking dog

or your father to protect you."

What? I spun around. My *father?* Was *he* here? And then I realized that Billy must have thought Uncle Arvie was my father. *What?* Had Billy Baker actually *seen* Uncle Arvie? I spun back around to ask, but he was gone.

"Beany booger," Uncle Arvie said again.

"Exactly," I agreed. "He likes to cause trouble."

Back in my room Uncle Arvie mentioned the second "please" when I opened my desk. He whisked his hand in the drawer and fluttered through it.

"What are you looking for?" I asked.

"Hammertoe." Uncle Arvie's fingers flickered through pencils and pens, paper and a ruler. "Nod hammertoe?"

"I don't know. What exactly is a hammertoe?"

"Hammertoe!" Uncle Arvie moved his hand in the air. "Hammer a needle. With hammertoe and needlinks."

I had absolutely no idea what he was talking about.

Suddenly, he shouted, "Ha! Hammertoe!"

"A *paintbrush*?"

"Hammertoe! Yin!" Uncle Arvie said. He rummaged some more, flipping out a twisted tube of blue oil paint. "Needlinks! Hammer a needle with needlinks!"

"You want me to paint a picture with the brush and paint?"

"Pin needle. Dinosaur flannelate," Uncle Arvie explained.

"*Your* picture? You want me to—to—what?"

"Flannelate!" Uncle Arvie was frustrated. He didn't know how to explain.

"Can't you show me?" I asked. "With the paintbrush and the paint?"

Uncle Arvie thought a minute. He took a piece of paper and placed it on the desk. Next he opened the paint tube and squeezed a drop onto the paper. He dipped the brush in the paint and started to draw, but an odd thing happened. There was paint on the brush, and the brush was moving across the paper, but the brush was leaving no marks.

"Hey!" I said. "Invisible paint?"

Uncle Arvie slammed his fist on the desk. "Nod fraggle." He dropped the brush and covered his face with his hands.

"Let me try." I dipped the brush in the paint and stroked it across the paper. "Look, it works for me." I painted a thin blue line across the paper, added a few strokes, and drew a house.

Uncle Arvie tapped at the picture. "Dinosaur needle." He jumped up, took the paintbrush, and pretended to paint a picture in the air. "Pin needle." Then he dropped the brush. "Nod flannelate."

"Not *finished*? Is that it? Your painting isn't finished?"

"Yin, riggle! Dinosaur flannelate!" Uncle Arvie shouted.

"Wait a minute," I said. "Let me get this straight. You've got a painting—an unfinished painting—and you want *me* to finish it?"

"Riggle!"

"I can't do that," I said. "I don't know how to paint."

Uncle Arvie held up my drawing of the house. "Dinosaur hammer," Uncle Arvie begged.

"Where *is* your painting?" I asked.

Uncle Arvie shrugged. He wasn't sure.

"Well, I guess we'll go back to your house tomorrow and see if we can find it. But I don't guarantee anything. Like I told you, I really don't know how to paint."

Uncle Arvie looked relieved. He cleared off the top of the desk. "Stamp!" he said, and he lay down on the desk and fell asleep. Bo curled up at the foot of the desk and he, too, fell asleep.

Uncle Arvie slept all day, and I was glad. It was very hard keeping up with a ghost who spoke his own language and asked for favors. I wondered where his painting was and how hard it would be to finish it.

That night, as I lay in bed, I remembered Billy Baker. If Billy really had seen Uncle Arvie, then

Billy, too, had seen a ghost. Wouldn't Billy be surprised to know that?

I stared out the window and searched the sky
for a bright star. When I found one, I wished for
my pepperoni.

6

HAMMERING THE NEEDLE

On Sunday morning I heard, "Dinosaur?" There was Uncle Arvie, floating near the ceiling again. "Good carpet, Dinosaur!"

"Good morning." I could smell pancakes, and it occurred to me that I hadn't seen Uncle Arvie eat since he had arrived. "Aren't you hungry?" I asked him.

"Nod."

"Do ghosts eat?"

"Nod."

"What do you do all day—when you're not visiting me, I mean? You don't eat. What do you do?"

"Stamp."

"Sleep? Is that all?"

"Nod." Uncle Arvie flapped his arms. "Mailer."

"Sleep and fly. I'd like that. Can you go wherever you want?"

"Nod." Uncle Arvie wiggled his arms and twirled and fell over. "Pailandplop."

"Oh, right. You can't steer. But you can aim, right? And then you just have to go where the wind takes you, right?"

"Yin."

Maybe that was why my father had not come to see me yet. Maybe he was aiming, but couldn't find his way.

"Dennis?" my mother called. She tapped at the door and came in. "You awake?"

Uncle Arvie smiled at her. "Feather macaroni."

"What *is* that smell?" my mother said. "It's so *familiar*, and yet—"

"Does it remind you of someone?" I asked.

"Yes, I think it does, but I can't exactly say who—"

Uncle Arvie jumped up and down. "Pin!" he said. "Pin! Pin!"

"So what are you and Bo doing today?" my mother asked.

"Hammer a needle!" Uncle Arvie said. "Dinosaur flannelate!"

"I thought maybe we'd go over to Aunt Julia's for a while," I said.

"That's good of you. She's so lonely now that Arvie is gone."

Uncle Arvie looked sad. "Pin Heartfoot. Pin sweel."

"I bet he's lonely too," I said.

My mother looked surprised. "But Dennis, he's in heaven. He won't be lonely."

"Maybe you don't stay in heaven all the time," I said. "Maybe sometimes you ride around on the wind all by yourself and—"

"Dennis, what an imagination you have!"

"Do you think my pepperoni is lonely?"

"Your *what*?"

"I—I meant Dad. Do you think he's lonely?"

My mother sat down on the bed beside me. "I don't know for sure, but no, I don't think he's lonely."

"I hope not," I said. "I hope he isn't lonely, but I bet he does miss us."

"I'm sure he does, Dennis." She stared at her wedding ring. "I miss him *terribly*. Most of the time I'm too busy to be lonely, but at night—"

"I know," I said. "At night it's harder."

After breakfast Uncle Arvie dusted off his boots and straightened his hat. "Pin mailer," he said, and he waggled his arms, lifted a few inches off the floor, and then came back down again. *"Foomf!"* he said. He waggled his arms again. Nothing happened. *"Foomf!"* Again he tried, and this time he lifted smoothly into the air and sailed through the window and over the trees, settling down in the grass across the road. At least he could steer for short distances, it seemed.

Aunt Julia was happy to see me and Bo again. "I love to have company," she said.

"Pin Heartfoot," Uncle Arvie sighed.

I said I had to use the bathroom. I knew the painting would not be *there*, but it would give me a chance to look in the bedrooms. I'd have to be quiet and quick about it, though.

I slipped into the spare bedroom and looked under the bed, behind the dresser, and in the closet. No paintings, except for one on the wall that looked completely finished.

In Aunt Julia's bedroom I checked under the bed and in the closet. I felt terrible, like a spy.

"Dennis?" Aunt Julia called.

I hurried back down the hallway to the kitchen.

"I thought maybe you got lost," she said, laughing.

I had an idea. "One time when I was here, I think I left something in your garage." I had to think fast. "Remember those little plastic dinosaurs I had? Do you think I could check if I left them here?"

"Your dinosaurs? I don't remember seeing them out there," she said. "But you can go look."

The garage was stacked with boxes, gardening tools, an old bicycle, and paint cans. When I asked Uncle Arvie how big the painting was, he held out his arms to show how wide and then swiveled them to show how tall.

"That's a pretty big painting," I said. "We shouldn't miss something that big." I poked around the boxes, moved tools, and searched the rafters. "It's not here. Can you think of anywhere else it could be?"

Uncle Arvie scratched his head. Suddenly he said, "Picket!" and pointed to the roof.

"I don't think a painting is going to be on the roof—"

Uncle Arvie pointed toward the house and then toward the roof. "Picket! Picket!"

"The *attic*?"

"Riggle! Picket!"

"Did you find your dinosaurs?" Aunt Julia called.

"No, I must have left them somewhere else." I was trying to think of a way to get into the attic. "Do you want me to do anything for you while I'm here?"

"Well, isn't that sweet of you," she said. "I can't think of anything—"

"Do you need anything taken up to the attic?"

"The attic? My goodness. I haven't been up there in *years*. I'm sure it's a complete mess. No, I don't think I need anything carried up there, though."

Uncle Arvie was sitting beside her, staring at her with a smile on his face. He liked to watch her.

"Maybe I could go up there and straighten it up for you." When I said this, I felt a little guilty, because my mother had asked me to clean *our* attic, and I was always finding excuses not to do it. "I like to poke around in attics," I added.

"What a lovely boy," she said. "If you're sure you want to, it's fine with me. Here, I'll show you where the ladder is."

The attic was dusty and crowded with boxes, old suitcases, a trunk, cast-off pieces of furniture, and plastic bags filled with blankets and clothing.

"I'll be down in the kitchen if you need me," Aunt Julia said from the foot of the ladder. Bo stared up at the hole through which Uncle Arvie and I had disappeared. He whimpered.

I moved boxes, clearing a space in the center of the attic. "I might as well straighten it up as I go," I said. I made a neat stack of boxes and piled the furniture against one wall. Then I dragged the plastic bags across the room and piled them on top of the furniture.

"I don't suppose you'd like to *help* me?" I asked.

"Nod middle—" Uncle Arvie tried to lift a box, but his hands went right through it.

"But you picked up a book—and a photograph—"

"Peasy!" He picked up a crumpled piece of paper and tossed it in the air. Then he kicked a tennis ball across the room. "Peasy!" But when he tried to move one of the suitcases, he couldn't.

"Too heavy?" I said.

"Yin."

So I moved the suitcases. They weren't *that* heavy, since they were empty. All, that is, except for the last one.

"Hey, something's in this one."

Uncle Arvie shouted, "Needle! Pin needle!"

Hurriedly, I unzipped the suitcase. Inside was a flat wooden box and a large object wrapped in brown paper.

"Needle! Pin needle!" Uncle Arvie said.

I unwrapped the object, and sure enough,

inside was a canvas. It was a painting of a blue sky with white puffy clouds, a blue-green lake, and rolling green hills. In the center of the lake was a rowboat with two people in it. A lady was sitting in the front, and a man was rowing.

But the painting was unfinished, just as Uncle Arvie had said. On the right side of the painting, in the lower corner, was a ten-inch patch of white canvas. It looked as if there should be another hill there, or more of the lake.

Uncle Arvie touched the people in the boat. "Pin and Heartfoot," he said.

It did look like Uncle Arvie and Aunt Julia in the boat.

"Wow, I wish I could paint like that."

"Dinosaur hammer," Uncle Arvie said.

"I don't know. I could never paint this well. Is this a real place?"

"Bunny room," Uncle Arvie said.

"It doesn't much look like a bunny room to me."

"Bunny room! Pin and Heartfoot. Bunny room!" He made kissing sounds with his mouth and showed me the gold ring on his finger.

"Honeymoon! This is where you went on your honeymoon, isn't it?"

"Yin, yin, yin! Bunny room!"

In the wooden box that was also in the suitcase, I found tubes of paint and paintbrushes. "Well, let's give it a try. What goes in this unfinished corner?"

Uncle Arvie touched a hill and a tree. He showed me how to mix two shades of green and one shade of yellow to get the right color. I worked slowly. I wanted it to look just right.

The grassy hill was fairly easy, but my tree looked sick. Uncle Arvie added some black paint to the brown that I was using, and very, very lightly, he placed his hand on top of mine, guiding my fingers slowly across the canvas.

"Wow," I said when we finished. "It looks like a real tree! I can paint! Well, with a little help. Now I guess it has to dry awhile, huh?"

Uncle Arvie held up three fingers and pushed one back down.

"Two hours?"

"Donkeys," Uncle Arvie said, waving his fingers. "Donkeys."

"Days?"

"Riggle! Donkeys!"

"Two whole days? That's a long time." I leaned the painting against the wall and dragged a box in front of it, to hide it but not touch it. "Is this for Aunt Julia? A present for her?"

"Yin. Pin needle a Heartfoot. Bunny room."

"She'll like it, I bet."

We heard the doorbell ring below, and then voices. Uncle Arvie listened carefully. Suddenly he flew down through the attic opening. "Beany booger!" he said.

7

BEANY BOOGER

Downstairs, Aunt Julia was saying, "Oh, how nice. I love chocolates!" She held a box of candy, and beside her stood Colin, smiling his silvery smile. Uncle Arvie stamped his foot.

"Would you like some coffee?" Aunt Julia asked, heading for the kitchen.

Uncle Arvie glared as Colin followed her down

the hall. Bo circled Colin, sniffing at his legs and growling.

"Shoo," Colin said. "Go away, dog."

"His name is Bo," I said.

Colin opened the chocolates and put the box on the table. Uncle Arvie leaned close. "Beany booger," he said as he reached in and pressed his fingers into the centers of five of the chocolates, crushing them.

Aunt Julia said, "Let me see these chocolates. I do love choc— Oh!" She stared down at the crushed candy.

Colin bent to look at the chocolates, too. "Hey—" he said, blushing.

"Oh, never mind," Aunt Julia said. "I'm sure the others are fine." She and Colin smiled at each other.

Uncle Arvie reached into the box and crushed five more chocolates.

"I'll have one of the others," Aunt Julia said, putting her hand into the box. "Ack!" she said, seeing the mashed candy.

"Hey," Colin said to me, "did you—?"

"I didn't touch them," I said, holding up my clean fingers as proof. "And neither did Bo. He hates candy."

Uncle Arvie pinched Colin's arm.

"Hey!" Colin shouted, slapping at his sleeve. "Hey!"

"Oh dear," Aunt Julia said, "not another wasp?"

Uncle Arvie pinched Colin's neck.

"Hey—" Colin slapped wildly at his neck and arms. "I gotta go!" He rushed to the door.

"Good biddle, beany bud booger," Uncle Arvie said.

"Goodness," Aunt Julia said. "I'll have to do something about those wasps." She picked up the box of candy, looked sadly at it, and threw it in the garbage.

Uncle Arvie seemed pleased.

"Did you finish cleaning the attic?" she asked.

"Not completely," I said. I knew we needed to wait two days for the painting to dry. "I'll come back on Tuesday and finish, okay?"

"Such a lovely boy," she sighed.

When Uncle Arvie, Bo, and I reached the park across from my house, Uncle Arvie said, "Mailer. Pin mailer." He flapped his arms, rose up in the air a few inches, and fell back to the ground. *"Foomf."*

"I guess it isn't always so easy," I said.

Uncle Arvie waggled his arms. Up he rose. He put one hand on his red cowboy hat to hold it on. He wobbled and flipped and rose far into the air.

"Be careful!" I shouted. "Don't get caught in the wind!"

Uncle Arvie somersaulted in the air. *"Oowee!"* he said. He flipped and turned and finally floated down until he was level with my window. "Good biddle—"

Quickly he flapped his arms, and in through my window he sailed.

Bo barked, and at first I thought he was barking at Uncle Arvie's flying. Then I realized he was barking at someone else. Billy Baker was riding toward me on his bike.

I wished I had a bike like Billy's. I'd asked for one for my birthday last year, but I didn't get one. I had started saving my allowance for one, but at the rate that was adding up, I'd be too old for a bike by the time I had enough money.

"Keep that stupid stinking dog away from me," Billy called as he spun around us. "Where's the geezer?"

"What geezer?"

"Your father—the geezer in the stupid red hat."

"He's not my father," I said. "And he's not a geezer."

"Oh yeah? Well, he looked like a stupid geezer to me," Billy said.

"He's a ghost."

"Sure he is, and I'm a piece of lettuce!" Billy grabbed my arm and squeezed it hard. "You stupid liar."

"He *is* a ghost," I insisted. My arm hurt like crazy.

Bo grabbed Billy's shoelace and pulled it.

"Get off," Billy said, kicking at Bo. "Get this stupid stinking dog off me."

"I'll get him off if you let go of my arm and listen to me for a minute—"

"Get the dog off first," Billy said.

"No, you let go of my arm first."

Billy let go, and I pulled Bo away.

"You've got one minute," Billy said. "Talk. And it better be good."

"It *was* a ghost you saw, and I can prove it," I said.

"Right. This I've gotta see." Billy was acting as if he didn't believe me, but there was something odd about that. It seemed as if he really *wanted* to believe me.

"See that house over there?" I said. "The ghost is in there right now. See that window? You wait here and watch. I'm going to ask the ghost to fly out that window. Then will you believe me?"

"What do you think I am?" Billy said. "Some

kind of idiot?" But he looked really, really interested.

"Just wait. You'll see." I raced across the street, with Bo following me.

I ran upstairs. "Uncle Arvie! Uncle Arvie—" I flung open my bedroom door, and there was Uncle Arvie, lying across my desk, sound asleep and snoring.

Outside, Billy Baker stared up at my window. "Wake up!" I begged Uncle Arvie. "Please!" I tried to shake him, but my hand wiggled through his arm. "Please, please wake up!"

Billy stared up at the window, waiting. When I tried to pat Uncle Arvie's face, my fingers passed through his cheek and under his nose. "Please, please, please, wake up!" But no matter what I did, I could not wake him.

I saw Billy pick up a rock. "Please, please, please," I begged Uncle Arvie. He snored. At last I said, "Come on, Bo," and went outside.

Billy tossed the rock up and down in his hand.

"So where's the stupid ghost?" he said.

"He's asleep."

"The ghost is *asleep*! Oh man, oh man. Maybe I should throw this rock through that window up there and wake him up."

Bo growled.

"Look," I said. "Really. I can prove he's a ghost. Meet me here tomorrow after school. I'm sure I can get him to fly then."

"Man oh man," Billy said. "I don't believe this. You must think I am stupider than you."

"Really," I said. "I *promise*."

Bo growled and snapped at Billy's shoe.

"Okay," Billy said quickly. "I'll give you one more chance. Tomorrow after school. Right here. And that stupid geezer ghost better fly, or you're going to see this here rock fly—right through your stupid window." Off rode Billy, still tossing the rock in one hand.

I sure hoped Uncle Arvie would fly for Billy. I sure hoped he would.

8
NOD MAILER

On Monday after school I dashed home, where Bo leaped on me, plastering my clothes with sloppy drools. My mother was still at work. "Come on, Bo," I said. "Let's get Uncle Arvie."

I was relieved to find Uncle Arvie awake. He was sitting on my desk holding a picture of his wife. "Pin sweel Heartfoot," Uncle Arvie sighed.

Through the window I saw Billy Baker riding his bike across the park, toward the spot where we had agreed to meet. "Uncle Arvie, I have a favor to ask," I said.

"A please?"

"Yes. I want you to show Billy Baker that you know how to fly."

"Pin mailer!" Uncle Arvie shouted, flapping his arms.

"Not yet." I led Uncle Arvie downstairs and across the street to where Billy Baker sat on his bike, his arms crossed over his chest. "So let's see him fly," he said. "I don't have all day, you know."

"Pin mailer?" Uncle Arvie said.

"What's he talking about?" Billy asked. "What's a *pin mailer*?"

"You'll see," I said. "Uncle Arvie, go ahead. Show him. Fly!"

Uncle Arvie straightened his cowboy hat and stretched his arms. He flapped them once, twice, three times. *"Foomf!"* he said. Again he flapped his arms, this time faster. Once, twice, three times. *"Foomf!"*

Billy said, "Oh man, oh man. *I* could fly better than *that*!"

"Wait," I said. "Sometimes it takes a while for him to warm up."

Billy looked at his watch. "Like I said, I don't have all day. He'd better hurry."

Uncle Arvie tried again. He wiggled and wobbled his arms. He flapped them up and down and waved them all around. He turned in circles. *"Foomf! Foomf!"* he grunted.

Nothing happened.

"Stupid geezer," Billy said. "Stupid dog. Stupid kid." He was trying to sound mad, but I had the feeling he was disappointed—as if he really wanted to see Uncle Arvie fly, as if he really wanted Uncle Arvie to be a ghost. He circled us on his bike. "Man, are you gonna be sorry," he said, and he rode off.

Uncle Arvie frowned. "Nod mailer." He looked pitiful.

Across the street my mother was getting off the bus. "Hi!" she called. "How was your day?"

"Terrible, just terrible."

"That bad? Well, come on in and tell me about it."

From the kitchen we heard a crash and a thud upstairs. In my bedroom we discovered the shattered window and, on the floor, a rock. Pieces of glass covered the carpet.

"Oh!" my mother said, looking out the window. "Who would do such a nasty thing?"

"Beany bud booger," Uncle Arvie said.

I wanted to tell her who had done it, but if I did, she might call Billy's parents. Then he'd *never* go away. "Maybe it was an accident," I said.

"Let's hope so," she said, but she didn't seem convinced.

9
NEEDLE FOR HEARTFOOT

On Tuesday we returned to Aunt Julia's house. She was just coming home from work and must have stopped for groceries on the way home, because she was loaded down with bags.

"Thanks," she said as I took the bags from her. "I wasn't sure you'd really come today. I thought you might forget."

She put her groceries away and sank onto the sofa. "I'm a little tired," she said. "I hope you don't mind if I put my feet up and take a little nap while you putter around in the attic?"

Uncle Arvie gazed at his wife. "Pin lalley, pin sweel, pin Heartfoot."

In the attic I hurriedly pulled the painting from its hiding place. "It feels dry to me. How does it look?"

Uncle Arvie stepped back and studied the painting. "Bunny room needle a Heartfoot! Feather bunny room!"

"You like it?"

"Feather, feather bunny room!"

"Don't you need to sign it or something?" I asked.

Uncle Arvie held up his hands. "Nod fraggle—"

"Oh right," I said. "I guess I could sign it for you, but then it would have to dry again." I smoothed out the brown paper that had originally covered the canvas. "Let's write something on the paper instead." I held my hand over the paper as Uncle Arvie guided me. *Pin Heartfoot,* we wrote.

"I'll just finish cleaning up, and then I'll give it to her, okay? That's what I'm supposed to do, isn't it? Give it to her?"

"Yin, riggle!" Uncle Arvie was really excited.

I finished stacking furniture and boxes against the wall, swept the room, and dropped a plastic garbage bag through the attic opening. Carefully, I eased the painting down through the hatch.

Aunt Julia was dozing on the sofa. I patted her arm. "Aunt Julia?"

"Oh!" she said. "Goodness, I was in dreamland! Are you finished already?"

"Yes," I said. "And I found something. I thought maybe it was for you. I didn't mean to be nosy. When I moved a suitcase, I heard this clunking sound, and just thought I'd look. This was inside. See? It says *Pin Heartfoot* on it."

Aunt Julia sat up quickly and put her hands to

her mouth. "What on earth—?" She ran her fingers lightly over the words *Pin Heartfoot*. "It's from Arvie."

Uncle Arvie sat beside her on the sofa.

"You haven't seen it before?" I asked.

"No, I haven't. What can it be?" She turned the package over and unsealed the edges of the paper.

Beside her, Uncle Arvie was grinning, and Bo thumped his tail.

Aunt Julia pulled the paper away and held the canvas in front of her. "Oh, oh, oh," she said. "It's our honeymoon. There's that beautiful lake, and look, there we are in the boat. That's me, and that's—oh, that's my Arvie."

Uncle Arvie's lip quivered.

"Do you like it?" I asked.

She sniffled. "Oh yes. Oh yes, I do." She stared at the painting. "I bet this was supposed to be my birthday present. I bet he hid it in the attic, and then— Oh, my Arvie."

Uncle Arvie leaned over and kissed her cheek,

and immediately she put her hand to her face. "Oh! I can almost *feel* him here with us right now." She sniffed the air. "Do you know—I can almost *smell* him here!" She laughed. "I bet you think I'm crazy, don't you?"

"No," I said. "Not a bit."

10

THIRD PLEASE

When we returned home after giving the painting to Aunt Julia, my mother was tap-ing a second piece of cardboard over the window. "Another rock," she explained, nodding at the glass on the carpet. "I've had enough of this. I'm going to find out who's doing such horrible things."

Later I said to Uncle Arvie, "We've got to do

something about Billy. He doesn't seem to care if he gets caught—which makes me think he's got something worse up his sleeve."

"Pin mailer," Uncle Arvie suggested.

"If only you could fly when I really *need* you to fly."

Uncle Arvie yawned. "Stamp!" He lay down across my desk. Within minutes he was snoring.

That night I stretched out on my bed and looked at the cloudy sky. I closed my eyes and imagined a clear sky with a single bright star, and on it I wished for my pepperoni.

I was awakened early the next morning by Uncle Arvie. "Good carpet, Dinosaur! Good carpet! Three please?"

There was a third favor to do for Uncle Arvie. "I've got school today," I said. "So it will have to be when I get home. What's the third please?"

"Dunder trampolink. Dunder boodled trampolink a gressapip."

"Hold on a minute!"

Uncle Arvie got down on his knees and scratched at the carpet. "Dunder," he said. "Dunder, dunder, dunder."

"You want me to clean the carpet?"

"Nod!" He pawed at the floor.

"You want me to dig something?"

"Yin! Yin! Dinosaur dunder!"

"Why? Where?"

"Trampolink boodled. A gressapip." Uncle Arvie pretended to dig in the carpet. Suddenly he stopped and stared down at the carpet. "Trampolink!" he shouted. "Boodled trampolink!"

"I don't know what you're talking about, and I'm late for school."

"Nod dunder?"

"Okay, okay, I'll dig for you, I guess. But I have no idea what I'm digging for or where I'll be digging. Can you explain to me after school?"

"Yin! Dinosaur dunder! Dinosaur dunder!"

At school that day, Billy Baker grabbed me in the hall. "That'll teach you to tell your stupid stories about stupid ghosts."

"Let go," I said, struggling against Billy's strong grip. "You wouldn't be so brave if your father knew about those rocks—"

"Oh yeah?" he said. "My father's *dead*. So there."

"Dead?"

"Yeah, dead. Now admit it: The geezer is not a ghost. The geezer is a geezer."

I struggled. "He *is* a ghost."

I was going to tell him that *my* father was dead, too, but he socked me hard on the arm. "Man oh man. Don't you ever learn? You'd better be in the park today at four o'clock. The geezer better fly then, or you won't have a single window left in your house. Got it?"

"I can't be there at four—I've got to dunder—I've got something to do." Billy squeezed my arm. "But I'll be there at six," I said.

Billy breathed in my face. "Yeah? Six? Okay, six o'clock, stupid."

All day long I prayed that Uncle Arvie would be able to fly that night at six o'clock, and all day long I wondered why Billy could see my ghost, but no one else could. Did it have anything to do with *foodle a doodle*? That's what Uncle Arvie had said when I asked why *I* could see ghosts: "Dinosaur foodle a doodle." Did Billy also *foodle a doodle*, whatever that meant?

After school, Uncle Arvie and Bo were waiting for me at the door of my house. "Dunder!" Uncle Arvie said.

So down the road we went. I hoped it wouldn't take too long, and that we'd be finished by six o'clock. I wasn't surprised to discover that we were headed for Aunt Julia's house again, but I was surprised to see, as we neared the house, someone leaving a box on the front steps.

Uncle Arvie clenched his fists when he recognized Colin.

"I was just leaving this for Julia," Colin said. "She's not home."

"I know," I said. "I'm going to—to weed the garden for her."

Uncle Arvie crept slowly up to Colin.

"Will you tell her I left this for her?" Colin said. "It's another box of chocolates. I'm sure *these* aren't smashed. I can't imagine what happened to those others. And I can't imagine why I keep getting stung by wasps when I'm here." He looked around quickly. "Do you see any?"

"Any what?" I said.

"Any wasps?"

"Well—" I said, as Uncle Arvie reached for Colin's arm. "As a matter of fact—"

"Ow! Hey! Ow!" Colin shouted, slapping at his arm. He ran down the walk and dived into his car.

"Beany, beany bud booger," Uncle Arvie said, kicking the chocolates into the bushes and heading for the garage.

While Uncle Arvie rummaged in the garage, I examined the old rusty bicycle I'd seen earlier, when we'd been looking for Uncle Arvie's painting.

It had loads of gears, a racing seat, and at least a dozen small pouches and compartments fitted here and there. But it was also rusty, the tires were flat, the chain hung loose, one pedal was missing, and the handlebars were bent.

"Dinosaur!" Uncle Arvie called. He had found a spade, which apparently was what he had been looking for. He motioned for me to bring the spade, and out to the back garden he marched. He walked slowly around, scratching his head. "Gressapip," he said, waving his arm across the bushes and flowers.

"Garden?"

"Yin, riggle! Gressapip!" Uncle Arvie continued walking around the flowers. At last he stopped in front of a rosebush. "Dunder!"

Bo tilted his head from one side to the other and whimpered.

"Here? You want me to dig up Aunt Julia's rosebush? Won't she be mad?"

"Dunder trampolink. Boodled trampolink a gressapip." Uncle Arvie jumped up and down and held his arms wide. "Trampolink! Boodled trampolink a gressapip!"

"Okay, okay, okay," I said. "I'll dunder the trampolink—whatever that is—here in the gressapip. But Aunt Julia's not going to like it when she sees her rosebush all dug up."

With his finger, Uncle Arvie drew a large circle around the rosebush.

Apparently he wanted me to dig all the way around the bush so I wouldn't chop its roots. I dug and dug, and all the while I kept an eye on my watch. I hoped we'd be finished by six o'clock.

II
DUNDERING TRAMPOLINK

For half an hour I dug. The rosebush was now lying beside the hole. Bo and Uncle Arvie were sitting on the grass watching me.

"Are you sure I'm digging in the right place?"

Uncle Arvie scratched his head.

"Can't *you* dig awhile?"

"Nod. Nod dunder." Uncle Arvie pushed the

spade against the ground with all his strength. It didn't even make a dent in the earth.

"Ghosts sure are peculiar," I said. "You can fly, but you can't dig. You can pinch, but you can't paint or write. You can lift little things, but not big ones. Very weird."

Bo jumped into the hole. He scratched at the ground with his paws, sending clumps of dirt flying into the air.

"Elephant dunder!" Uncle Arvie said.

"Good old Bo, you're a good old digger."

"Dennis? Is that you?" It was Aunt Julia, home from work.

"Uh-oh," I said. "Now we're in trouble."

"What in the world—? What *are* you doing?" She stared at her toppled rosebush and at the hole where Bo was still digging. "Dennis, I hope you have an explanation for this—"

I thought. "Well, I—" I thought some more. "I had this dream—"

"What sort of dream?"

"In this dream, I saw Uncle Arvie—"

Aunt Julia gasped. "*My* Arvie?"

"Yes, and he told me to dunder up the gressapip—and that seemed to mean I should dig up the garden, right here."

"Under my favorite rosebush?"

"Well, yes," I admitted.

"Do you know why it's my favorite rosebush?" she asked.

"No."

"It's because it was a present from Arvie. He planted it here with his own hands, three years ago."

"Oh. I'm sorry I dug it up," I said, glaring at Uncle Arvie, who was sitting on the grass watching her. Bo was still scratching away at the hole, flinging dirt.

"I don't understand why you would have a dream about Arvie telling you to dig up my favorite rosebush."

Bo barked. He leaped out of the hole and pulled at my jeans.

"What is it?" I asked. "Quit pulling me." Bo barked and leaped back into the hole, scratching at the dirt.

"Wait a minute," Aunt Julia said. "What's that?"

In the center of the hole was a piece of green metal. I reached in and brushed away the dirt, uncovering more green metal and a brass handle. "It looks like some sort of box," I said. With the spade I loosened the dirt around the box.

"It *is* a box," Aunt Julia said.

I slipped the spade under the box and lifted it out of the hole. It was not a very big box, but it was heavy.

"Trampolink!" Uncle Arvie said. "Boodled trampolink!"

"Buried treasure?" I said.

"Riggle!"

"Is it locked?" Aunt Julia asked.

I brushed the dirt away. There was a small brass latch at the front, and it wasn't locked.

12

BOODLING CHINKAPINK

"I feel very peculiar," Aunt Julia said, sinking to the grass. She sniffed the air. "This is very strange. Very, very strange. You'd better open the box, Dennis. I can't."

Inside the box was a bundle of letters tied with brown string. "What on earth—?" she said. She touched the top letter. "These are letters I wrote

to Arvie before we were married. He *saved* them?"
She lifted the bundle from the box, and as she did
so, she revealed what was beneath the letters.

"Trampolink!" Uncle Arvie said.

Beneath the letters were bundles of money and
rolls of coins.

"Money!" I said. "Treasure! Trampolink!"

"Why, look at all this money," Aunt Julia said.
"Hundreds, thousands of dollars." She covered her
face with her hands.

"Don't cry," I said. "I'm sure he didn't steal it."

"That's not why I'm crying. I *know* Arvie didn't
steal this. He saved it. For years and years and
years."

"But why didn't he put it in the bank?" I asked.

"Arvie? Put money in a *bank*? He didn't believe
in banks," she said. "After he died, I found little
bits of money hidden everywhere—in his shoes,
in his jackets, in our dresser. I knew there had
to be more money somewhere, but I had no idea
where. And I had no idea it was this much! Just

think, if you hadn't had that dream—"

She grabbed me and squished me in a hug. "What a miracle! I'm going to call your mother right now and tell her what you've found. Goodness, goodness, goodness!"

As I started refilling the hole with dirt, Uncle Arvie said, "Boodle chinkapink?" He and Bo ran across the grass and toward the front of the house. When they reappeared, Bo was carrying the box of chocolates that Colin had brought earlier. "Boodle chinkapink!" Uncle Arvie said. Bo obeyed by dropping the box of candy into the hole.

"Okay, boodle the chinkapink!" I said. I covered the box of chocolates with dirt, replaced the rosebush on top of it, and spread more dirt around the bush.

"Chinkapink a gressapip!" Uncle Arvie said.

On the way home I felt terrific. Buried treasure! And Aunt Julia seemed so happy. She hadn't even counted the money yet. She had seemed more excited at finding the letters, and when I left her, she was sitting at the kitchen table reading them.

As we neared home, Uncle Arvie said, "Pin mailer?"

Without thinking, I said, "Sure, go ahead."

Uncle Arvie wiggled his arms and flew into the air.

"Oh no!" I cried. "Wait!" I looked at my watch. It was almost six o'clock. Billy would be waiting.

13
MAILER, MAILER

A strong wind was blowing through the park when I reached it. Leaves whipped through the air. I wondered if I had time to go home first and get Uncle Arvie. I was afraid he'd go to sleep again, and I wouldn't be able to wake him.

But it was too late. Billy Baker was riding toward me, pedaling fast, and he looked angry.

He squealed to a stop and jumped off his bike. "Man oh man, it sure is windy," he said. The wind blew his hair in wild tangles, making him look even more threatening. He grabbed my collar and snarled, "So where's the geezer, stupid?"

I strained to look across the road at my house. I thought I saw something move in the window upstairs. Was it Uncle Arvie?

Billy threw me to the ground and knelt on my chest. "Repeat after me: 'The geezer is a geezer.'" Billy's hands pressed against my arms.

"He isn't—" I said. "He isn't a geezer. He's a ghost."

Billy twisted my wrists. He said, "If the geezer is a ghost, then that means he's dead, right? So how come my father isn't a ghost?"

"My father's dead *too*," I said. "And maybe—"

"Liar!" Billy said. "Liar!"

I squirmed and twisted, trying to get loose. A flicker of red flashed in the air above us. "Look— up there—"

"Don't try to pull that one on me," Billy said. "You're just trying to distract me."

"Really, look, up there—"

Billy turned quickly. "Where?"

"There, above the road—coming this way—"

Billy gasped. "Jeez—"

Uncle Arvie was flying.

"Holy moly," Billy said.

I twisted beneath him and rolled free.

The wind whipped the leaves through the air, and Uncle Arvie rose and somersaulted and dived and soared. *"Oowee!"* Uncle Arvie shouted. "Mailer! Mailer! *Oowee!*" Uncle Arvie twisted and turned and looped.

"H-h-holy m-m-moly!" Billy cried.

Uncle Arvie swept past Billy's face.

"H-h-holy m-m-moly!" Billy shouted. "He *is* a ghost!" For the first time since I'd met Billy Baker, he grinned. He actually grinned.

Uncle Arvie flew above the tree and dived again, narrowly missing Billy's head. A strong blast of wind blew through the park. *"Oowee!"* Uncle Arvie said, as the wind caught him and carried him far into the air. "Pailandplop!" he shouted. "Pailandplop!"

"Uh-oh," I said, watching Uncle Arvie rise higher and higher. "He can't steer—"

"Where's he going?" Billy asked.

"Pailandplop, pailandplop!" Uncle Arvie said, but his voice was fainter and fainter as he sailed toward the clouds.

"Come back!" I shouted. "Come back!" I ran across the park, following Uncle Arvie, trying to keep him in sight.

A thin echo drifted down: "Good biddle, Dinosaur, good biddle—"

"Oh please," I called. "Try! Try to steer—"

But the wind was too strong. It pulled Uncle Arvie up into the clouds, and I could see him no more. I stood for a long time watching the sky, hoping to see that red cowboy hat.

There was nothing more to be seen. Uncle Arvie was gone.

I walked back across the park, passing Billy, who was still staring at the sky. "He *is* a ghost!" he repeated. "He *is* a ghost!"

"Told ya—" I said.

My mother and Bo were standing in the backyard. "Dennis!" my mother said. "Where have you been? Aunt Julia called and— What's wrong? Is something the matter?"

I looked up into the sky once more and then knelt beside Bo. I whispered into Bo's ear: "Uncle Arvie flew away."

Bo cocked his head and whimpered.

"Dennis?" my mother said.

"Why are you out here?" I asked. "It's a little windy, isn't it?"

She wrapped her jacket tighter around her. "It sure is. But I was just thinking—after Aunt Julia called and told me about you finding the money Arvie had buried—I was just wondering."

"Wondering what?"

"Do you think your father might have buried

something back here? The way Uncle Arvie buried something in *his* garden?"

"I don't know."

"Oh well, it's probably a silly idea," she said. "Let's go inside. I have some good news for you."

14
A Wish

"It's really Aunt Julia who has the good news," my mother said.

I felt terrible. All I could think about was Uncle Arvie, who had disappeared on the wind.

The phone rang. "Go on," my mother said. "Answer it. I bet it's Aunt Julia."

Reluctantly, I lifted the receiver.

"Dennis? Is that you?" Aunt Julia said. "Did you happen to see a box of chocolates on the porch when you were here? Colin just phoned and said he left a box of chocolates."

"Well, I—"

"I'm not suggesting that *you* took them!" Aunt Julia said. "Anyone could have taken them. It was silly of him to leave them there in the first place."

"Yes, well—"

"I'm beginning to think he's rather a silly man. All that business with the wasps. *I* never saw any wasps, did you?" she asked.

"No, I—"

"Exactly. I think Colin is imagining things. He's a foolish man. Not nearly as interesting as your Uncle Arvie was. Colin is sort of a—a—"

"Sort of a beany booger?" I said.

"You sound just like Arvie," Aunt Julia said. "Thank you for reminding me of him. And thank you for finding Arvie's poem, and that beautiful painting of our honeymoon—" She sniffled. "And of course for finding the box today with all my letters and the money. I don't know how to thank you—"

"Oh, that's okay," I said.

"I think you deserve a reward," she said. "Anything you want. Anything at all. It's yours. What would you like?"

I thought. There were three things I wanted, but I knew that Aunt Julia could not give me two of those things. So I asked for the third.

I said, "In your garage is an old bike. Was that Uncle Arvic's?"

"That old thing?" Aunt Julia said. "That old rusty thing? Sure, it was Arvie's, but—"

"I have a little money saved to fix it up, but I don't have enough. Maybe you could help me get it fixed—?"

Aunt Julia said, "Of course I could. We'll get new tires and have it painted and— Are you sure that's what you want? You could have a whole new bicycle if you'd rather."

I was tempted to say, "Yes! A new bike!" but I thought about all those secret pouches and compartments on Uncle Arvie's old bike. "I'd rather have the one in the garage." Maybe some of Uncle Arvie would be in it—something magical and mysterious in a ghostly sort of way.

That night, in bed, I listened to the wind rattle against the cardboard taped to my window. I knew that Billy Baker wouldn't be throwing any more rocks. I wondered if Billy could see a ghost because he wanted a ghost. Needed a ghost. Maybe that's what *foodle a doodle* meant. Maybe Billy and I both needed a ghost—we both foodled a doodle.

Across the room was my empty desk. I wished Uncle Arvie were lying across it, with his red hat poking off one end and his legs sticking straight out off the other end. That was one of the things I wanted that Aunt Julia could not give me.

Uncle Arvie was probably far, far away now, sailing along on the wind, going wherever it took him. I found one bright star and made my wish. I wished for the other thing that Aunt Julia couldn't give me.

"Maybe this wind will bring more ghosts," I said. "Maybe this wind will bring me and Billy our pepperonis."

It *could*, I thought. This wind *could* bring our fathers sailing right through our windows. You never know about ghosts.

The Boy
on the Porch

I

The young couple found the child asleep in an old cushioned chair on the front porch. He was curled against a worn pillow, his feet bare and dusty, his clothes fashioned from rough linen. They could not imagine where he had come from or how he had made his way to their small farmhouse on a dirt road far from town.

"How old a boy is he, do you think?" the man asked.

"Hard to say, isn't it? Seven or eight?"

"Small for his age then."

1

"Six?"

"Big feet."

"Haven't been around kids much."

"Me neither."

The man circled the house and then walked down the dirt drive, past their battered blue truck and the shed, scanning the bushes on both sides as he went. Their dog, a silent beagle, slipped into his place beside the man, sniffing the ground earnestly.

When the man and the dog returned to the porch, the woman was kneeling beside the old cushioned chair, her hand resting gently on the boy's back. There was something in the tilt of her head and the tenderness of her touch that moved him. He wondered if they would have their own child one day. No, no, time enough to think about *that*. No need to rush things.

2

The young couple, whose names were Marta and John, were reluctant to go about their normal chores, fearing that the boy would wake and be afraid, and so they took turns watching over the sleeping boy. It did not seem right to wake him.

For several hours, they moved about more quietly than usual, until at last John said, "It is time to wake that child, Marta. Maybe he is sick, sleeping so much like that."

"You think so?" She felt his forehead, but it was cool, not feverish.

And so John and Marta made small noises: they coughed and tapped their feet upon the floor, and they let the screen door flap shut in its clumsy way, but still the child slept.

"Tap him," John said. "Tap him on the back."

And so Marta did, tapping him lightly at first, and then more firmly, as if she were patting a drum. Nothing.

"Lift him up," John said.

"Oh, no, I couldn't. You do it."

"No, no, it might scare him to see a big man like me. You do it. You're more gentle."

Marta blushed at this and considered the child and what might be the best way to lift him.

"Just scoop him up," John said.

And so Marta did just that. She scooped up the boy in one swift move, but he was heavier than she had expected, and she swayed and turned and flopped into the chair with the boy now in her arms.

Still the boy slept.

Marta looked up at John and then down at the dusty-headed boy. "I suppose I'd better just sit here with him until he wakes," she said.

The sight of his wife with the child in her lap made John feel peculiar. He felt joy and surprise and worry and fear all at once, in such a rush, making him dizzy.

"I'll tend to the cows," he said abruptly. "Call me if you need me."

Her chin rested on the child's head; her hand pat-patted his back.

"It's okay," Marta whispered to the sleeping child. "I will sit here all day, if need be."

Their dog normally shadowed John from dawn until dusk, but on this day, he chose to lie at Marta's feet, eyes closed, waiting. Before John went to the barn, he scanned the drive again and circled their farmhouse. Finding nothing out of the ordinary, he hurried on to his chores.

Marta closed her eyes. "It's okay, it's okay," she whispered.